Halfway Through the Holidays

A WEST TINDALE SHORT ROMANCE

ELLE WHITTAKER

LEMONADE
HEART
PRESS

ISBN (e-book): 979-8-9909996-4-0

ISBN (paperback): 979-8-9909996-9-5

*For anyone who's ever been overwhelmed,
especially over the holidays*

One

CORINNE

Corinne leaned her head against the cold porcelain of the toilet bowl. She felt a little better, but not by much. Waves of nausea still rolled through her.

I don't have time for this, she thought. *It's five days before Christmas.*

From outside the bathroom, she heard a thud, and then the unmistakable cry of her two-year-old son. Then the whining voice of her seven-year-old.

"Mooooom!"

Corinne closed her eyes and took a deep breath.

"Tyler, can you check on the kids, please?" she called out. Nothing. "Tyler?"

The cries got louder. For a toddler, Mason had a hell of a pair of lungs. And Emily was the loudest seven-year-old on the planet. Corinne clenched her jaw. Apparently, her husband was "too busy" to help with the kids.

As usual.

Corinne stood up and rinsed out her mouth, then opened the bathroom door. Both of her children were hanging from her limbs within seconds. Corinne could barely understand what the cause of their fight was, but she didn't care. It was probably something dumb anyway.

"Emily, go get your brother's ipad," she said. "Get yours, too." It wasn't until both of her children were settled on the couch (five feet away from each other) with their screens that the house became quiet enough to think.

Corinne could hear her mother-in-law's voice in her head. *Screen time will rot their brains! They should be outside! Whatever happened to board games?!*

Well, if Vivian had had her kids in the 2010's or later, she would have known that screens make the best babysitters. And seven-year-olds and two-year-olds couldn't exactly play board games together.

Corinne sank into an armchair and tried to breathe. She still felt slightly nauseous. She hoped whatever was happening would pass quickly. Maybe it was something she ate…? She absolutely did not have time to get sick.

She glanced around the living room. There was a pile of unfolded laundry on the floor. Along with every single one of the toys her children had. And half of the toys the dogs had.

Shit, the dogs.

Corinne stood and waited for another wave of nausea to pass before she made her way to the back door. Sure enough, Pickle and Lulu were both waiting patiently to be let out. There was at least four feet of snow in the backyard, but both golden retrievers bounded out anyway. Corinne stood shivering in the doorway, then called them both back in.

They ran through the kitchen before she had a chance to wipe their paws, and they left a trail of wet pawprints on the linoleum. Probably onto the carpet, too.

Corinne avoided looking at the pile of dirty dishes in the sink, the food-covered high chair, the crusted-on yogurt and god knows what else on the table. Because if she looked at it, she was going to scream. She closed her eyes. Where the hell was her husband?

Honestly, he was probably doing some stupid chore that absolutely did not need to be done in preparation for his family coming to town. They were arriving in four days, and he had probably decided to clean out the gutters or something. Change the oil in the car. Powerwash the shed. He'd done it before. It was his way of claiming that he was being helpful. Last year when Corinne had asked him to help clean the kitchen in preparation for family visiting, he had re-caulked the bathroom sink.

It was so good in the beginning. They'd known each other their whole lives, and building a life together felt so natural.

There were some hard years when they first started the West Tindale Adventure Company. It was way more complicated than either of them realized to run a tour company that did both river rafting trips and horseback rides. The amount of equipment purchases and insurance paperwork and park permits was overwhelming. The logistics of it all made them wonder, more than once, if this was a good idea.

But they were doing it together. They had sex on the floor of the office on late nights. They would order Chinese food from Zhao's and work into the wee small hours of the morning, and Corinne would look up at Tyler sometimes and he would look back and the two of them would smile.

He had such a great smile. It made her feel like they could do anything. That, and Tyler was so dedicated. When he got started on a project, he was the hardest worker Corinne had ever known. And he never complained—he just kept working in his laid-back way. In moments when things felt challenging, his steady, cheerful attitude made it all feel easier.

And then, after a few years, West Tindale Adventure Company finally started turning a profit, and they made a down payment on a house on Outpost Way, and went through an entire deck of Kama Sutra cards in three months.

When Emily came along, she was tiny and curious and perfect. Watching Tyler become a father made Corinne fall in love with him all over again. It was like all the love she had felt for him before had expanded, filling up every corner of her soul. Becoming a mother had rearranged her entire self, on a cellular level, and every single one of those cells was filled with more love for her little family than she could have imagined.

Emily hadn't slept for the entire first year of her life, and Corinne couldn't think straight most of the time, but Tyler was still there, walking the floor at night with Emily screaming in his arms. In the afternoon light, he would toss their daughter up into the air to make her laugh, and by the time she was four, she was such an angel that they decided to have another one.

Mason had come two weeks early, which was enough to scare them but not so much that he needed a ton of help. Apparently having two kids was a completely different beast than having one, but they still managed. Tyler was still present as a father, but he and Corinne were both so exhausted that there were days when they barely spoke to each other before collapsing into bed.

Was that what happened to my marriage? Corinne thought. *Was it having two kids?*

Or maybe it was her. Fatherhood had made Tyler more attractive, but motherhood had just made Corinne feel haggard and old. She'd given up shaving her legs years ago, and her belly sagged slightly from where her skin had stretched to accommodate two babies. She was no longer the hot nineteen-year-old he had married. (Maybe they had gotten married too young? Nineteen was an insane age to get married. Who had let them do that?!)

Corinne made her way back into the living room and sank into one of the couches. The piney scent of their freshly cut Christmas tree wafted through the air, which Corinne knew should feel magical, but it just made her feel slightly sick. She was tempted to reach out and unplug the lights that twinkled in the boughs, but that felt childish, so she pulled out her phone instead. She thought about texting Tyler to ask where he was, but she was too annoyed with him. So she texted her best friend Bri instead.

> CORINNE: Tyler's entire family is coming into town in four days and I have no idea where he is and also I have a stomach bug.

> BRI: Oh shit what?

Corrine sat and thought for a moment.

> CORINNE: I think my marriage might suck.

Bri didn't answer for a minute, and Corinne was worried that she had sounded too serious, and then she worried that she didn't sound serious enough.

> BRI: Want me to come to town?

Tears flooded Corinne's eyes. What had she done to deserve such a perfect best friend? The thought of Bri coming to town, helping her clean the kitchen, and playing with her kids, filled her with so much gratitude that she thought she might burst.

But then the logistics caught up with her. The house was about to be filled with people, and Bri had her own extended family in Utah. Corinne couldn't ask her to drop everything and come take the one spare bedroom they had (and take it away from her parents-in-law) just because she was feeling a little overwhelmed.

> CORINNE: This offer made me cry. But I'll be okay.

> BRI: What would be most helpful to you right now?

Corinne sighed.

> CORINNE: Honestly? For my husband to act like he was still in love with me. For my kids to not be monsters. For me to feel like a human being. Like a woman, and not like just a mom. I can't remember the last time I felt like someone wanted me for something other than opening a bag of fruit snacks.

> CORINNE: But I know you can't exactly help with any of those things.

> BRI: If ever I need a bag of fruit snacks opened, I'll do it myself.

> CORINNE: Thanks. Love you.

> BRI: Love you, too. And seriously, call me if you need. Even if I don't end up coming to town, I can still just talk on the phone. And if you want me to give Tyler a good talking to, I can do that, too.

CORINNE: You're the best.

"Mama?" Emily said.

Corinne sighed and looked up from her phone. "Yes, baby?"

"Mason pooped."

Corinne closed her eyes for one moment, and then got up to grab a clean diaper.

Two

TYLER

Tyler pulled the grocery bags out of the car. He'd wanted to go down to Silver Falls to get stuff, since there was a better selection, but the roads were pretty bad, and he wanted to save the gas. He stepped into the kitchen and set the bags down.

Corinne walked in and frowned. "Did you go to the store?" she asked.

"Yeah, I wanted to grab a few more things before people come into town." Tyler started opening cupboards to put snacks away.

"Could you text me next time you're going to go somewhere?" Corinne asked. "Or, you know. Tell me?"

"Oh, sorry," Tyler said, glancing at his wife. "I thought you heard me."

"Why did you get more toilet paper?" she asked.

"Because people are coming over," Tyler replied. "I wanted to make sure we have enough."

"I already got extra," Corinne replied. "Did you check the closet before you left?"

Tyler shook his head. "Well, now we have extra extra. We should be good for Thursday."

"You mean Saturday?"

Tyler turned and looked at Corinne. "No? Thursday?"

His wife stared at him. For the first time that morning, he noticed that she was looking a little pale. She looked tired, too, but they had two kids and one of them was a toddler—being tired was just part of this stage of life.

"Your family is coming into town on Saturday," Corinne said, sounding slightly panicked. "Four days from now."

"They changed their flight," Tyler replied. "Didn't you see the text?"

Corinne shook her head. Tyler pulled out his phone and scrolled through his messages. "Yeah, last week," he said. Then he noticed that he and his mom were the only ones on the thread with that update. He frowned. "Oh," he said. He looked up. "Did my mom not text you?"

Corinne leaned her hands on the counter and bent her head. He could see her taking deep breaths. Finally, she looked up at him. "Are you telling me that your entire extended family is coming into town the day after tomorrow? All seven of them?"

"Yeah?"

Tyler was honestly feeling confused. Sure, it was a couple days earlier, but they didn't have any other plans. It couldn't make that much of a difference, could it?

But his wife was looking at him with rage in her eyes.

Which he knew should concern him. But when she got intense like this, it was actually kind of…hot?

He'd always loved the fire in her. All throughout high school, he would watch her on the soccer field, determined and strong. She was so powerful somehow. He kind of wandered through life, but Corinne got shit done. It was her hard work and stubbornness that had made the West Tindale Adventure Company work. He never could have done it without her. Sure, right now his wife was in her pajamas with her brown hair in a messy ponytail, and yesterday's mascara smeared under her eyes. But when that fire shone through, he was helpless. Without even thinking about it, Tyler took a step toward her.

But Corinne raised her hands to stop him. "Tyler," she said. "This is…I can't believe this."

"Why?" he asked. "It doesn't really change too much, does it?"

She raised her eyebrows at him. "Doesn't change much? Do you realize how much we have to do today and tomorrow now?"

Tyler thought through all the things they might need to do before family came into town. Corinne had washed all the sheets and pillowcases last week, so those were ready. And they had extra towels. And they had plenty of food in the house. And now toilet paper.

"There's not much else to do, is there?" he asked.

Corinne's eyebrows rose even higher and she glanced around the kitchen. "Are you standing in the same room I am? This whole kitchen needs to be cleaned. And the living room. And the bathroom. We don't have meal plans in place. We need paper plates and garbage bags and bottled water and shampoo and like, fifteen other things. We still have to wrap presents, for god's sake."

"That's not that hard, though," Tyler said. "We could—"

But he stopped because Corinne had just put a hand over her mouth. Suddenly, she turned and bolted out of the room. A few seconds later, he heard her retching.

Oh no.

Corinne was sick. Maybe that's why she looked so pale.

This might also be why she was upset.

He glanced at the kids in the living room, each of them with an ipad on their lap. Emily had headphones on, but Tyler could hear the high-pitched sound effects of whatever show Mason was watching. He walked toward his and Corinne's bathroom.

Corinne was kneeling in front of the toilet, looking exhausted.

"Corinne?" Tyler asked. "Hey, are you okay?"

She looked up at him. "Do I look like I'm okay?"

The question felt like a trap. "I…don't really know how to answer that," he replied honestly.

Corinne doubled over the toilet again, and Tyler fell to his knees beside her, rubbing her back. *I guess this is marriage*, he thought. It was a lot of other things, too, but in his mind, these were the moments that really counted.

Corinne spit into the toilet and then flushed. She stood up, shrugging his hand off her back. She leaned over the sink to rinse her mouth out.

"Was it something you ate?" Tyler asked.

"Who fucking knows?" Corinne replies. "I have a toddler. Kids are germ factories."

"Can I do anything for you?"

Corinne glanced at him in the mirror. Something passed over her face, some expression he couldn't quite read. She shook her head.

"Are you sure?" Tyler asked. "If you make me a list—"

"I don't want to have to make you a goddamn list!" Corinne exploded.

Tyler blinked at her. Corinne rarely lost her temper. She got heated, sure, but he couldn't remember the last time she'd yelled at him like this. She really must be feeling sick. And if he put himself in her shoes, then he got it. If he was feeling sick, and he suddenly found out his in-laws were coming into town two days earlier, he'd be upset.

"Hey, I'm sorry," Tyler said. "I'm sorry you're sick. And I'm sorry about not telling you about the date change. I honestly thought you knew."

But Corinne just shook her head. "It's not just the date change," she said. "Or being sick."

"It's…not?"

Corinne stood gripping the bathroom counter. Tyler studied her face in the mirror, but it was a long moment before she looked back at him.

"It's everything, Tyler," she said. "It's the kids, and the food stuck to the kitchen table, and you not checking to see if we had toilet paper before going out and buying more toilet paper, but still not getting more of the things we actually need."

"I was trying to be helpful," Tyler replied. He could hear the defensiveness in his voice, but he was feeling defensive.

"I don't want to have to be your manager, Tyler," she said. "I want to…" To Tyler's surprise, tears filled her eyes. "I want to be your *wife*," she continued.

Her words went straight through his heart. She was clearly hurting, and he couldn't figure out what to do to stop it. But he also couldn't figure out what she meant by being his "manager." And as for being his wife…

"Corinne, every time I try to touch you, you scoot to the farthest side of the bed."

She huffed out an incredulous laugh, then raised her hands to cover her face. After a few moments, she swiped at her tears and grabbed a tissue. "I can't do this right now," she said. "We just have to get through the holidays."

"Can't do what right now?" Tyler asked.

She turned and faced him. "Is this seriously working for you?"

"What?"

"This," Corinne replied, gesturing between the two of them. "Our marriage."

"Corinne, I literally just rubbed your back while you threw up."

She looked at him. Then nodded, her face unsmiling. "Right," she said. "I guess we'll talk about this after Christmas."

"I don't even know what we're fighting about right now!"

"Don't worry about it," Corinne said. "We'll just get through Christmas."

"I can help with—"

"Right," Corrine cut him off, walking past him to exit the bathroom. "I'll make you a list."

Tyler walked out of the bathroom, then sat down on the bed.

If his marriage was in trouble, it was news to him. Which made him feel dumb, but in his defense, why didn't she say anything before now? Maybe she didn't mean it? Maybe she was just extra irritable because of being sick, and not knowing about the change of plans. He'd be irritable if he were put in that situation.

But this seemed like more than just irritation. She'd just asked him if their marriage was working for him. Which it mostly kind of was? It's true that they didn't have sex as often as he would have liked, but that was just life with kids, right?

Tyler took a deep breath. Whatever was going on, he could fix it. He'd do everything on whatever list Corinne made and he'd shovel the driveway and change diapers. He'd be husband of the year this Christmas.

He was determined to try.

Three

CORINNE

Corinne opened her eyes and sat up experimentally. She hadn't thrown up any more yesterday, and she was feeling okay now. Maybe whatever it was had passed. She glanced over at Tyler's side of the bed. It was empty.

They hadn't really spoken for the rest of the day after their fight the day before. She'd been too annoyed by him.

It wasn't just that their marriage sucked. It was also that he didn't seem to *notice* that it sucked. And he'd made that awful comment about her scooting to the far side of the bed every time he tried to touch her.

Of course she wanted him to touch her! But he always tried when she was exhausted or when they hadn't said a word to each other all day. It was hard to feel "in the mood" when sex was just a perfunctory fifteen-minute event in the dark. And that's what it was, every three weeks or so. Nowadays Corinne was better at taking care of things on her own.

Corinne stood and made her way into the kitchen. Mason and Emily were both up and…was that…an entire carton of eggs? On the floor?

Corinne took a deep breath. It was. Both Mason and Emily were giggling, sliding their hands through the slimy yolks on the linoleum.

"Okay, we're done with the eggs," Corinne said, grabbing a paper towel. She pulled Mason to his feet only to realize that he was stepping in the mess with his footie pajamas. She shook her head in frustration, then unzipped Mason. He stood in the kitchen in his diaper while Corinne stopped Emily from rubbing more eggs on her hands and arms.

So now not only did both kids need a bath, first thing in the morning, but now she had to go out and buy more eggs. They'd need at least a dozen to feed everyone breakfast tomorrow, unless they did cereal, but that was way more expensive.

Tomorrow, Corinne thought. Her in-laws were coming *tomorrow.* It's not that she disliked her in-laws. She got along well with Tyler's parents, even though his mom could be a little judgmental. She was pretty good friends with her sister-in-law, Tyler's brother's wife. It's just that the house wasn't ready for ten additional people, no matter how much she liked them.

"Emily, stay here," she said. "I'm going to go put your brother in the bath. Don't touch the eggs anymore."

Corinne carried Mason to the bathroom, pulled off his diaper, and set him in the tub. Within minutes, Tyler had carried Emily in and started washing her hands in the sink.

"What happened?" Corinne asked.

Tyler looked up at her. "The kids wanted to help," he said.

"We should clean up the eggs before they dry in the kitchen," Corinne said.

Her husband paused and looked at her. "Do you want me to bathe the kids or clean up in here?"

Corinne closed her eyes. She wished he would just… take initiative. It really was like managing an employee. She didn't care which job he did. She just wanted him to pick one. And if she was being completely honest, she didn't want to do either task.

Actually.

"You can do both," Corinne said. "I'm going to go get breakfast in town."

She didn't even change out of her pajamas. She just threw a coat and boots on and climbed into the car. Sullivan's was still open this time of year, and she needed a cup of coffee and maybe a baked good. And to be away from her family.

Maybe it was unreasonable for her to leave Tyler on his own with both the kids and the mess in the kitchen. But if she were home on her own, that's what she would have to do. He would just have to figure it out.

Corinne parked on Silverview Way and climbed out of the car. She was sure she looked like a mess, but she was too exhausted to care.

A welcoming bell rang as Corinne pushed the door to Sullivan's open. She was greeted by walls in a dark, rich navy, complemented by long yellow curtains. Christmas lights twinkled along the perimeter of every window, and pine wreaths hung on all the walls. One enormous fresh-cut tree stood in the corner, decorated with popcorn strings and bows. Corinne could faintly hear Ella Fitzgerald singing about a sleigh ride. The place was mostly empty… Kenny from the library was sitting on one of the couches, and Maya stood behind the counter. She glanced up when Corinne walked in.

"Coffee or tea?" she called out.

"The most sugary coffee you can come up with," she replied. She and Maya had known each other since high school, and even if they didn't hang out that often these days, it was nice to have a girlfriend in town. Corinne strode to a table by a window and sat down. She stared out at the dirty snow until Maya brought a mug over. She also set down a plate of banana bread.

"Oh, I didn't order this," she said.

"I know," Maya replied. "I brought it out for you anyway."

To Corinne's embarrassment, she felt her eyes sting with tears. This small gesture from someone she'd known for almost her whole life was about to unravel her.

"Oh, hey, shit," Maya said.

"I'm fine!" Corinne cried, but her voice wobbled.

Maya sat down across from her and reached out to take her hands.

"Do you want to talk about it?"

Corinne sighed shakily. "I think my marriage sucks. And I don't know when I stopped feeling like a person, but lately I'm just…someone's mom. Like, constantly. I want to be Tyler's *wife* again. If he can manage to be a husband."

Maya looked at her thoughtfully for a moment.

"Sorry," Corinne sniffled. "That's a lot."

"It's fine," Maya replied. She paused, and then said, "This is going to sound insane, but have you ever made a 'want list'?"

Corinne brushed a tear away. "Moms don't get to make wish lists. We just read them."

Maya smiled softly. "Not like a Christmas wish list. Well, kind of. But just…list what you want."

Corinne huffed out a watery laugh and then reached out to grab a slice of banana bread. "What's the point? The things that I want feel impossible. My husband sucks and I don't think I can change him."

"Just write it anyway," Maya said. "You'd be surprised.

Maybe you'll learn something you didn't realize before, and writing it out can be its own kind of magic. Here."

Maya stood and then walked to the counter. She brought out a notepad and a pen, then placed it in front of Corinne. "First of all, your coffee and banana bread are on the house. Second of all, just try it," she said. "Trust your friendly West Tindale witch. Or count it as a magical Christmas wish. Write what would happen if your wildest dreams came true." Maya smiled and walked back to the counter.

Corinne shook her head, but she picked up the pen anyway.

She didn't even know where to start. She took a sip of her coffee (which was wonderfully sugary) and stared out the window. *If my wildest dreams come true,* she thought. Then she put pen to paper.

1. I want Tyler to sweep me off my feet. Again. Somehow.

Corinne raised her head. Okay, well, if it was literally anything, then:

2. I want Mason to be potty-trained.

And then suddenly, the wants were flowing out of her, filling the page.

3. I want Tyler to kiss me like he wants me.

4. I want to have the hot young body I had before I had two kids.

5. I want my kids to not fight literally all the time.

6. I want my house to be clean.

7. I want to laugh with my husband.

8. I want my minivan to not be filled with crushed up cheerios and books and toys and crusty mystery stains.

9. I want Tyler to look at my body and treat it the way he did when we were first dating.

10. I want

Corinne paused. She felt self-conscious writing the next part, but Maya said to just write it out.

10. I want Tyler to shove me against a wall and like, have his way with me. I want to feel how desperate he is for me. Maybe there are even people over or something, but he just can't wait. Like I'm so hot that I'm driving him crazy and if he can't have me right now he's gonna die.

11. I want Tyler to take it very very very slow. No kids who need us outside the bedroom door and nowhere to be the next day. I want

him to touch every single inch of my body like it's sacred. To treat me like a work of art.

As Corinne wrote, she felt something unfamiliar and heated stirring inside of her. She swallowed.

She didn't expect to spend the morning writing out her erotic fantasies while sitting in Sullivan's Coffee. At the encouragement of one of her high school friends. Corinne wasn't sure if this is what Maya meant when she said "just write what you want." But if Corinne dug down into the wants she carried, she found desire for her husband there. It was just that she couldn't get to it. Not with the piles of dirty dishes and the stretch marks and the diapers and the "make me a list" requests.

Corinne finished off her drink, and took a last bite of banana bread. Then she folded the list up and put it in her jacket pocket. She didn't think any of the things on the list were very likely to come true, but Maya said just making the list was magic. And Christmas is supposed to be magic.

"Thanks, Maya!" Corinne called out. "For everything!"

Maya lifted a hand in a wave.

Corinne didn't exactly feel ready to go back home, but her in-laws were coming tomorrow, and there were things to do.

Four

TYLER

Tyler heard the front door open as he got the kids dressed. He waited for Corinne's voice to greet them, but she just went straight to their room. Once the kids were ready, he turned on an episode of Bluey in the living room and went to clean up the egg mess in the kitchen.

He scooped up the empty carton and piled broken eggshells into it. He had what he thought was a brilliant idea of using a spatula to kind of scrape egg off the floor, but he only succeeded in spreading egg even more. How would Corinne do this? Maybe he should ask her.

No. He was going to be husband of the year. He could figure this out. It took him two rolls of paper towels and a good fifteen minutes to finish cleaning, but he did it without help.

On his way back inside from taking the trash out, Tyler noticed Corinne's jacket on the floor by the back door. He picked it up and lifted it to the hook, but as he did so, a piece of paper fell out of one of the pockets. He bent to pick it up, and was about to return it to its place when he noticed his name written on it.

    1. I want Tyler to sweep me off my feet. Again. Somehow.
      2. I want Mason to be potty-trained.
      3. I want Tyler to kiss me like he wants me.

Holy shit.

He wanted to be husband of the year, and here was an actual instruction manual about how to do it! He scanned the rest of the list. There were a few more things about having a clean house and car and their kids not being so difficult. But his eyes lingered on the things on the list that included his name. Reading about the things his wife wanted him to do to her…he felt those words in both his chest and his groin.

He'd never really shoved Corinne up against a wall. It just hadn't really occurred to him. But now that he had read it, it was all he could think about.

He'd had a crush on Corinne for as long as he'd known her. He'd taken other girls on dates, and even had crushes on them, but his heart had belonged to Corinne since before he even understood what it meant to have your heart belong to someone.

They'd grown up together, but he decided she was the girl for him when they were in second grade. They must have been…what? Seven? (The same age his daughter was now, he realized with a start.) Tyler and Corinne were seated next to each other in their second-grade classroom, and Corinne had opened her pencil box to show him a collection of bugs she'd gathered from the playground during recess. He'd looked up at her mischievous grin and decided right then and there that he was going to marry her. On their wedding day, as he stood across from her and said his vows, he could hardly believe his luck.

He heard Corinne coming out of their room, so he snapped a quick picture of the list on his phone and stuffed it back into the jacket pocket.

"Hey," she said.

"Are you feeling better this morning?" Tyler asked.

Corinne nodded. "I made a list," she said.

For a moment, Tyler froze. Was she about to tell him about the list he had just found? Then he remembered their fight from the night before and guilt squeezed his chest.

"You didn't have to," he started.

"Well, I did," Corinne replied, not looking at him. "But I'm not going to make assignments. Just pick something and start doing it. I'm going to start meal planning and then I'll make a grocery list."

"Don't forget to add eggs," Tyler said, smiling. He was trying to make a joke, but Corinne didn't laugh. Instead, she set her list down on the counter, walked to the kitchen table and sat down with paper and pen.

Tyler picked the list up and scanned it. Clean kitchen. Clean bathroom. Meal plan. Wrap presents. Go to store for food and other supplies. Snow-blow drive-way/street.

"I'm gonna snow-blow the driveway," Tyler said. Corinne looked up at him, then glanced toward the living room.

"Can you be done in like, an hour?" she asked. "So that you can watch the kids while I go to the grocery store?"

"No problem, babe," he said.

He saw something flash behind her eyes when he called her "babe," but it was gone as soon as he noticed it.

TYLER LACED up his boots and threw his beanie on. There wasn't too much snow in the driveway, but they needed to make sure there was enough parking along the street for everyone, and that was going to take some doing. While he pushed the snowblower in careful lines, he thought more about Corinne's list. There was one thing that was confusing him.

A third of the things on the list were things about wanting him. Or wanting him to want her. But this same thing had come up when they fought yesterday—the fact that she always turned away when he tried to initiate something. He knew they had young kids and that didn't exactly mean a robust sex life, but if Corinne really wanted him, why didn't she act like it?

When Tyler pushed the snowblower back into the garage, he moved past the minivan and had a thought. He pulled his phone out and looked at the picture of the list he had found.

8. I want my minivan to not be filled with crushed up cheerios and books and toys and crusty mystery stains.

He grinned to himself. "Husband of the year," he said quietly.

He hauled all of the trash out of the minivan, and made a pile of the toys and books and other random junk that had ended up in the seats. He ran the shop vac along the floorboards, in every corner. It really was impressive how much of a mess kids were capable of generating.

Maybe I'll try to like, seduce Corinne at the Christmas party, he thought. He wasn't totally sure how to do that, but there was that list item about his wife wanting them to sneak away at a party. Maybe that's what their sex life needed. A little excitement.

Tyler was starting to wipe down the dashboard when he heard his name. He looked up to find Corinne frowning in the doorway.

"Hey," he said, smiling. *Mark number eight off your list,* he thought.

"What are you doing?" Corinne asked, her frown still etched deep.

This was not the reception Tyler had been expecting. Didn't she want the minivan clean? Why wasn't she happy?

"I'm um…I'm cleaning out the minivan," Tyler said.

Corinne closed her eyes and took a deep breath. When she opened them, she looked at her husband with the same patient, infuriated look on her face that she sometimes gave the kids. "That isn't on the list," she said.

Tyler wasn't sure what to say—he had a gut feeling that he shouldn't mention the *other* list he had found. "I know," he said. "But it needed to be done, so I thought—"

"What happened to watching the kids?" Corinne cut him off. "I need to go to the store."

Tyler stood and blinked at his wife. Shit. He had completely forgotten. He had been so excited about giving Corinne the gift of a clean minivan that he'd literally forgotten about the other thing he'd told her he would do.

"Shit," he said. "Corinne, I'm sorry. I can totally watch the kids."

Corinne folded her arms. "Unless you wanted to do some other useless chore right now."

This time Tyler frowned. Yes, he'd messed up, but that had felt mean. "I said I'm sorry," he said.

His wife stared at the ground. "Thank you," she finally said quietly. "I'm going to the store. Emily and Mason need lunch."

"Got it," Tyler said.

As he made sandwiches for the kids, he thought about his mistake. It seemed really obvious now. Of course the minivan was an extra thing that didn't need to be done right now. The whole house still needed cleaning. And he'd said he'd watch the kids after snow-blowing and then forgotten about it.

Okay, he thought. *This just means I can't mess up the rest of Corinne's secret wish list.*

While the kids ate, he studied the to-do list his wife had left him. And then he studied the other list she'd written and left in her jacket pocket.

When they'd gotten married, he'd promised to do everything in his power to make all of her dreams come true. It was only fair, since marrying her had been *his* dream come true. There were a few things on the list that he didn't have the power to do (instantly potty train Mason, for example, or prevent their kids from ever fighting). But he could help make everything else happen. By this time tomorrow, he'd sweep Corinne off her feet. He'd make this the best Christmas they'd ever had.

Five

CORINNE

Corinne stood in her bathroom and stared at the faint pink line.

"Shit," she whispered. "Shit shit shit shit."

She couldn't even believe she still had a pregnancy test laying around. Mason was two, and she and Tyler had been using condoms since he was born.

Mostly.

When another wave of nausea had rolled through her this morning, right in the middle of an extended family breakfast, Corinne had felt a sense of deja vu. This didn't feel like sickness nausea.

This felt like pregnancy nausea. And now that she thought about it, she hadn't had a period in a minute. She'd just been so stressed about the holidays she hadn't noticed.

So Corinne had dug through the medicine cabinet and pulled out a pregnancy test, and in another moment of deja vu, had waited anxiously for the results to be ready.

And there the results were. Pregnant.

Right when Corinne fully realized that her marriage was falling apart, she was pregnant.

What the hell were they going to do? Could they even afford another kid? Emily and Mason were so much work already, and Mason wasn't potty-trained and Corinne refused to have two different sizes of diapers in the house at the same time. Corinne did some quick math in her head. She had no idea how pregnant she was, but no matter what, the baby would come in the summer. Right during the busy season for their business. The idea of trying to manage the West Tindale Adventure Company while enormously pregnant made Corinne want to crawl into bed forever.

And what about Tyler? What about the growing distance between them? Tyler wasn't a bad father, he was just a…dumb one? And also a dumb husband?

Corinne's stomach clenched with guilt at the thought. She felt like a 90s sitcom wife, calling her husband dumb. It felt like she was leaning on a bunch of tropes that she absolutely hated.

But the man had spent yesterday morning cleaning out the minivan when the entire house needed to be prepared for visitors.

It was true that the clean minivan was nice. Corinne thought she probably shouldn't be as grumpy about it as she had been. It was just that he did a lower priority chore instead of a higher priority chore.

"Corinne?"

Tyler's voice came from the other side of the bathroom door, and Corinne quickly wrapped the pregnancy test in toilet paper and hid it in the trash.

"Yeah?" she called out.

"Just checking on you," Tyler said. "Are you feeling okay?"

"I'm fine. I'll be out in a minute."

Tyler paused, then said, "Okay." She heard his foot-steps as they departed. Corinne wiped her tears away and prepared to rejoin the family.

∾

THE LIVING ROOM was complete chaos. As Corinne knew it would be. But it felt more overwhelming this year than in past years. Tyler's mom and dad were in town, as well as his brother and his wife, and their three kids. Tyler's uncle had also somehow ended up being invited, and brought along his teenage son and daughter. The house that normally held four people and a few pets was currently holding fourteen people. Everyone had just finished lunch, and the kids were in the living room, screaming, while the grown-ups were cleaning up the kitchen.

Corinne caught a glimpse of Tyler lifting a box of paper plates and cups, and felt a faint zing move through her. Because his arms looked really good? And the sight of him being helpful was hot. Corinne shook her head. Must be the pregnancy hormones.

Tyler glanced up and caught her eye and smiled hesi-tantly. And Corinne couldn't help it—she smiled back. What the hell were her emotions even doing right now? She was still pissed at him for a lot of reasons, but she and Tyler had known each other for so long and been through so much together. He was a dumbass, yes, but she couldn't help but feel the tiniest bit of warmth toward him.

He stepped around the kitchen island toward her.

"Hey," he said quietly.

"Hey," Corinne replied.

"I have something for you. Do you have a minute?"

Corinne raised her eyebrows, but followed him to their

room anyway. When they were away from the chaos of the rest of the house, Tyler pulled an envelope out of his pocket. "I got you this. It's an early Christmas present. Sorry I was dumb about the minivan earlier."

The warmth Corinne had felt in the kitchen grew to a glow in her center. Maybe it was the pregnancy hormones again, but his apology made her want to cry. It didn't fix everything—not even close—but it was meaningful anyway. "Thank you," she whispered.

She took the envelope from out of his hands. She opened it and pulled out a slip of paper.

One year membership to Planet Fitness, Silver Falls location.

Corinne frowned, then looked up at Tyler. "What… what is this?" she asked.

"It's a gym membership," he said, smiling. "I got one, too. I know you've talked about wanting to get your body back to pre-baby…status, so I thought we could go to the gym together!"

"The gym in Silver Falls," Corinne said. She had meant for it to be a question, but it came out flat.

Tyler shrugged. "We don't have one in West Tindale."

Corinne stared at him. "You got me a gym membership for a town two hours away. As a Christmas present."

"Yes?"

Any warmth Corinne had felt for this man had evaporated the moment she read the words on the slip of paper. She didn't even know what to say to him. There were so many things wrong with this "present" that she didn't even know where to start. The inconvenience of a gym membership to a place an hour away? The need for childcare while they both went to the gym? The fact that driving to Silver Falls was almost impossible for half the year? The implication that her body needed improving somehow? The fact that he gave her a gift that was literally *more work*?

Corinne couldn't think of a single thing to say. So she simply set the paper down on the dresser and walked back out into the living room.

She couldn't even bring herself to be all that surprised or angry. She just felt a vague background irritation. It was just her dumb husband being dumb. As usual.

For the rest of the day, Corinne played with the kids and chatted with her in-laws and picked up plates and refilled cups and smiled and smiled and smiled. Her mother-in-law had offered to make dinner for everyone that night, so Corinne focused on setting the tables.

She and Tyler hardly crossed paths all afternoon.

Dinner was more smiling and talking. When Tyler's brother Justin offered to pour her a glass of wine, she blinked at him for a moment, then declined. "Still feeling a little yucky from that stomach bug," she explained. She figured she could use that excuse for the next couple of days. Now did not feel like the time to announce a pregnancy.

Sometime after dessert, Tyler stepped over to where Corinne was sitting on an armchair in the living room, chatting with Justin's wife Angela. He held his hand out to her.

"Come here," he said.

Corinne looked at him blankly for a moment, and then took his hand.

He led her down the hallway, the sounds of the family fading. "What do you need?" Corinne asked.

When they got to their bedroom, Tyler shut the door behind him.

Then he shoved Corinne against it.

Corinne gasped in surprise. Tyler buried his face in her

neck, kissing her in that sensitive spot he always knew how to find. And in spite of everything from the last few days, it filled Corinne's entire body with fire.

"What are you—?"

But Tyler cut her words off by slanting his mouth over hers.

Holy shit.

He hadn't kissed her like this since...had he ever kissed her like this? Corinne could hardly get her bearings. Tyler pressed his hips into her, pinning her harder against the door, her shoulder blades pressing into the wood. His lips left hers again, this time to move down her jaw, nipping her earlobe with his teeth. Corinne's breath hitched in pleasure.

Tyler's hands moved down her body, and she was being swept away in sensation, no time to think or question any of it. But then his hands pressed into her belly, and Corinne's thoughts snapped into place.

Her belly. Where there was currently a tiny soon-to-be person, one that Tyler put there, and that he currently did not know about. The belly that Tyler thought needed improving with a gym membership.

Corinne placed her hands on Tyler's shoulders and pushed him away.

They were both breathing heavily, staring at each other in the dim light of their room. Tyler reached down to adjust his pants, and Corinne's eyes moved down to the hardness there. When she looked back up at his face, she could see the heat in his eyes.

"What are you doing?" she asked.

Six

TYLER

"I'm…I'm trying to kiss you," Tyler replied. He took a hesitant step toward her. "And maybe more…"

"There are people over," Corinne replied. "Like, a lot of people."

Tyler gave his wife a sly smile. "I know," he said. He took another step toward her. "That's what makes it hot." He leaned forward and ran his nose along the side of Corinne's neck. "Isn't this what you wanted?" he whispered.

But Corinne put her hands on his chest and pushed him away. She folded her arms and glared at him. "What the hell made you think this is what I wanted?"

Tyler was confused. He had found this exact scenario on a list of things that his wife wanted. Shoving her against the wall while people were over was literally one of the things she had written. And now she…didn't want it?

"I thought…" he started.

Corinne's frown had caused all of the heat to melt out of the moment. Even though…god, even when she was upset, she was pretty.

Tyler closed his eyes. He might as well come clean. "I found your list," he said. "In your coat pocket. You had listed all of these things that you want. So I thought…"

He trailed off as he looked at his wife. To his surprise, tears welled in her eyes. "Hey," he said quietly.

Corinne covered her face with her hands and shook her head. The sight made Tyler feel so helpless that he wanted to crawl out of his own skin. He took another step toward her and rested his hands on her shoulders.

"Hey, hon," he said. "I'm sorry. Just…tell me what to do."

Corinne let out a sob, and it broke Tyler's entire heart.

"Babe," he said quietly. But when he tried to gather her into his arms, she pushed him away. She swiped at her tears angrily.

"I'm going for a drive," she said. "Tell the family whatever you want." And then she stepped out of the room, slamming the door behind her.

Tyler sat down on the bed with a thump.

What the hell was he doing wrong? Why wouldn't his wife just *tell* him what she wanted? None of it made any sense. Hell, even when he found a list of what she wanted, and thought he was following it, she just kept getting farther away from him.

He collapsed backward and stared at the ceiling. He thought back to their fight in the bathroom earlier, when Corinne asked if their marriage was working for him. And suddenly, with a leaden weight, he realized just how high the stakes were.

Maybe this wasn't just a rough patch.

Did this mean…what did this mean? He tried to picture it, the unspeakable thing lurking in the back of his mind. Finding an apartment of his own. Shuffling the kids back and forth. Trying to run the business together.

Tyler sat up.

No.

He had loved Corinne for his entire life, and he was going to fight for her.

When Tyler exited the bedroom, the rest of the house was still chaos, with kids yelling and grown ups attempting to have conversations. Tyler stepped into the kitchen to see his brother pulling the full trash bag out of the can.

"You don't have to do that," Tyler said.

"I know," Justin shrugged. "I just saw that it needed to be done."

"Thanks anyway," Tyler said. He grabbed a fresh bag from the cupboard and put it into the empty can while Justin tied the full bag closed. Tyler sighed. He felt guilty about his brother doing the things that should be his job as host.

"What's the sigh about?" Justin asked.

Tyler looked up, then pointed to the full trash bag in Justin's hands. "This is the kind of thing I wish Corinne would just tell me."

"To take out the trash?" Justin asked.

"Yeah," Tyler replied. "I keep telling her to make me a list."

Justin stopped and looked at his younger brother. "Tyler," he said. "Where do you think Corinne gets the list?"

Tyler opened his mouth, then shut it again. Then repeated the motion. Because that thought had literally never occurred to him before. "I guess...I guess she makes it?"

"And how do you think she makes it?"

"I guess she thinks of what she wants done, and then she...makes the list."

Tyler had the embarrassing feeling that he was missing

something, like there was some obvious fact that Justin understood and that he didn't. It made his collar feel too tight. Justin looked at him for a moment longer, then said, "Grab your coat. Let's go for a walk."

"I thought you were taking out the trash."

"We can do that on the way."

The air was bitingly cold, but after Justin threw the trash in the bear-proof bin on the corner, the two men started walking down the street. Tyler was turning their conversation over in his head, trying to find the thing he wasn't getting. Finally, Justin broke the silence.

"Do you think there's a difference between what Corinne wants done and what needs to be done?" he said.

Tyler thought for a moment. "Sometimes," he said. "I think…I think I'm afraid of messing up. I literally did that the other day. I cleaned the minivan when it didn't *need* to be done. But I thought she *wanted* it done."

Justin nodded. "I used to do shit like that all the time. Sometimes I still do. But Angela was the one who told me to just look around and do what needs doing. Like the trash. It needed to be taken out, so I took it out."

"But what if I do the wrong thing?" Tyler asked. He felt like an idiot even having this conversation, but then he thought of Corinne's pained expression in their bedroom and swallowed hard.

Justin shrugged. "Then you do the wrong thing. But it's really not that hard to figure out. Like, I'm sure the minivan did need cleaning. But with people coming over, how much of a priority was that?"

"Right," Tyler said slowly. Something was clicking into place in his brain.

"With the trash," Justin continued, "You know it's a priority, because if it's not done, then there's nowhere to put trash. The minivan can survive if no one cleans it for another week."

Tyler thought for a few minutes, listening to the sound of his boots crunching in the snow. "I found this list," he said eventually. "Of things Corinne wants. Some of them were…well, some of them were none of your business, but the others, it was stuff like having a clean house and a clean minivan. But I…when I tried to give her the things on the list, they kept being the wrong things. A few days ago, she said she wanted to be my wife, and not my manager, but I don't know what that means. I kept…I don't know what—"

To his shame, his voice caught. Justin stopped and threw his arm around Tyler. They walked like that for a few feet.

"If you were co-COOs of the household," Justin said, "what would you do?" When Tyler didn't answer right away, he added, "You own a business together. How do you manage things there?"

Tyler stopped dead in his tracks.

"Holy shit," he said.

Because all of it had just fallen into place. There was almost an audible click as he realized what was missing from his marriage. Corinne didn't want an employee, she wanted a partner. And she might want to feel like a "wife" in the bedroom, but of course she didn't want to have sex with him when he was doing things like ignoring the full trash can.

"I'm an idiot," Tyler said.

Justin smiled at him. "I've been saying that for years."

"What do I do?"

Justin swung them around so that they were walking back toward home. "You're a co-manager," he said. "You'll figure it out."

By the time they got back to the house, the chaos had died down a bit. Someone had put a Christmas movie on for the kids, and the adults were chatting in the kitchen. Corinne was still gone, and Tyler felt his chest ache at the thought of his beautiful, smart, capable wife crying alone somewhere. But now he had a plan. A real one. Not an "employee of the year" plan but an actual "husband of the year" plan.

There was still a chance that he would mess this up. That his problem-solving skills were still useless. But he felt more clarity than he had in a long time. His perspective had shifted. He glanced around the room and started gathering dishes while his plan took shape. He pulled out his phone and sent a few texts. Then he walked over to his mom.

"Hey," he said.

"Hey, honey. Where's Corinne?"

Tyler swallowed. "She's um…she's on a drive. Could you…how would you feel about having the grandkids to yourself for the next couple of days?"

His mom raised her eyebrows. "I'm thinking about taking Corinne up to a friend's cabin," Tyler said. "As a Christmas present. I still have to run it by her, but I wanted to make sure the kids would be okay."

"I'd be happy to watch them," his mom replied. "And it's not like I won't have help."

"Thanks, Mom," Tyler said. Then he started on the dishes.

Seven

CORINNE

Somehow, Tyler and Corinne managed to not speak to each other for the entire rest of the night. Corinne was asleep before Tyler even got into bed.

But now it was morning, and Corinne didn't even want to think about the long, exhausting day ahead. She didn't want to think about the dozens? Hundreds? Of kids in her house. Or her family. (Tyler's family, really.) Or the meals that would have to be prepared and served and then cleaned up after. Corinne sat up and waited for a wave of nausea to pass.

Oh yeah, there was also that. Being pregnant. She closed her eyes, but opened them again when Tyler stepped into the room.

"Hey," he said.

Corinne glanced at the suitcase he was holding in his hand and frowned. "Are you going somewhere?" she asked.

"If you want to," Tyler replied. "We could go somewhere." He sat on the edge of the bed. "How would you like to get out of here for a few days?"

"Tyler," Corinne said, sighing. "We can't just leave in the middle of our family Christmas."

"I know it's not ideal," Tyler replied, "But I just got the feeling that all of this was a lot. So I talked to my parents and asked if they'd watch the kids for the next two days, and then I texted Sean about using his family's cabin. If you want to, we can head up there for a couple of days and be back in time for Christmas morning."

Corinne blinked at him. That actually sounded… amazing. A quiet place away from all of the chaos, where she didn't have to be a mom, or a host.

"What about food?" Corinne asked.

"If you want to go, I can stop by the store and grab everything we need," Tyler said.

Corinne was very afraid that she was about to burst into tears. Because she was exhausted and she wanted to escape and her husband was stepping up for the first time in years. Was this even real?

"Am I dreaming?" Corinne asked.

Tyler smiled at her. "You're not dreaming. Do you want to go?"

Corinne took a deep breath. "What will you tell everyone?" she asked.

Tyler shrugged. "That my Christmas gift to you was a break." His eyes roamed over her features, and Corinne was suddenly aware of her smudged mascara and tangled hair. But Tyler didn't seem to be noticing those things. He was just…looking at her, a soft smile on his face.

Corinne threw the blankets off. "Give me fifteen minutes to pack," she said.

She started toward the closet, but Tyler grabbed her hand from his seat on the bed.

"What?" Corinne asked.

Tyler gazed up at her, and then pulled her into him so

that she was standing in between his legs. He reached up and tangled his hand into her hair, then brought her face down to his and kissed her. It was slow, familiar, and soft. He tasted like maple syrup.

When he pulled away, Corinne couldn't help but smile at him.

WITHIN AN HOUR, Corinne and Tyler were headed into the park toward Sean's family cabin. It was about an hour drive, and as soon as they were alone together, Corinne didn't know what to say. She'd known Tyler almost her entire life, and they'd been married for a decade, but she'd spent the last few months being so mad at him that he felt like a stranger. She stared out the window.

"What are you thinking about?" Tyler asked.

Corinne glanced at him. His hair fell over his forehead as he looked over at her. For a second, it was like they were teenagers all over again, him driving her to some spot in the park where they could fool around in the backseat until curfew.

"You," Corinne answered honestly.

Tyler smiled, but it was an anxious smile. "In a good way, or in a bad way?" he asked.

Corinne thought. "Both," she replied.

Tyler frowned, then turned the blinker on.

"What are you doing?" Corinne asked. They were miles away from the cabin, and there was nothing but walls of snow on the side of the road.

Her husband pulled the car over and brought it to a stop. He put the hazard lights on and turned toward her.

"Corinne," he said.

"What?"

"I've been a dumbass," he said.

Corinne let his statement hang in the air for a moment. "That's true," she said. "But can you be more specific?"

Tyler turned to look out the front again. "I've been… god, Corinne, I've been a fucking child. I just expected you to take care of everything, and I thought I was being a good husband, but I think I get it now. I think I understand what you meant when you said you wanted to be my wife, not my manager. Babe, I'm so sorry." Tyler turned back and his eyes were so sincere that Corinne couldn't do anything but stare at him.

She sat in stunned silence for what was maybe five minutes. "What…what happened?" she asked.

Tyler sighed, and looked up at her through his lashes in that way that drove her crazy. "Honestly, Justin had to talk some sense into me."

"What did he say?"

Tyler smiled. "I won't get into all of it, but he talked about the business, and how running a house and a family is similar. And I realized that I've been a shit employee of the Young Family. But I want to do better. No, I *am* doing better. And you don't have to teach me how. Just…I just need you to let me try. I'm going to pay attention to when the dishes need to be done and help potty train Mason and make my own lists."

Corinne looked at her husband. And it was like all of the longing she could have been feeling for him for the past six months erupted inside of her. She unbuckled her seatbelt and leaned across the center console to grab his collar and kiss him hard.

Tyler made a little noise of surprise, but it soon melted into a moan of hunger. Corinne felt him reach up and cup her jaw, his lips moving against hers. Then his hands were roaming over her, and suddenly Corinne had way too much clothing on. She unzipped her jacket so that Tyler could slip his hands inside, move his palms up her ribs. Corinne fumbled at his seatbelt until it was released, then pulled him closer to her.

He reached up and cupped one of her breasts. "Is this okay?" he gasped between kisses.

Corinne responded by grabbing his other hand and moving it so that he was holding both of her tits. He moaned into her mouth.

The spot between Corinne's legs was aching, and she wanted Tyler's hands there, or his thigh, or his cock, or his mouth, anything—she wanted as much of him covering as much of her as possible, and she wanted most of him right there. She let out a little whimper of frustration, her hips shifting. She reached down to Tyler's zipper and found him hard and straining against his jeans.

"Corinne, honey," Tyler said, his voice hoarse. Corinne leaned forward to kiss along his throat, her hand moving over his erection. "We gotta—Jesus—we gotta get to that cabin or I'm going to…fffffuckkk…"

Corinne smiled against Tyler's skin. She was drunk on the power she had over him, knowing that she could drive him crazy. "Then get us to that cabin," she whispered. Then she scooted back to her seat, and barely had time to buckle up before Tyler peeled out into the road.

She looked over at him, his hair mussed, his eyes a little wild. He was still breathing heavily, and the ache in her sex intensified. When he glanced her way, it was almost more than she could stand. Slowly, experimentally, she reached down between her legs, her eyes still on her husband.

Corinne brushed her fingers over the fabric of her

leggings, already damp with longing. Then she spread her hand and pressed hard against herself.

Tyler looked over at her and his eyes widened. "Are you…insane?" he said, his voice ragged. "How am I supposed to…drive? When you're…God, Corinne, this is…"

Corinne bit her lip and let her eyes fall closed, fighting a grin. She lifted one leg and let her knees fall open even wider, her fingers still moving over her sex. She could feel her breath getting faster.

"Corinne," Tyler said, his voice sounding strangled.

Corinne opened her eyes and looked at him. One of his hands was on the steering wheel, and the other was pressed firmly over the bulge in his jeans.

"You've got to let me…" he said. "Just let me…get us to the cabin. Safely. Please."

Corinne grinned and removed her hand, letting her knees fall closed again. "As long as you're trying to do it safely," she said.

They drove in silence for a few moments, Corinne studying Tyler's face. The bulge in his jeans wasn't getting any smaller, and she watched as he swallowed hard.

"What are you thinking about?" she asked, feeling just a tiny bit wicked.

He glanced over at her, then refocused on the road. "You've never…" he started. He swallowed again. "You've never let me watch."

Corinne's confidence took a tiny stumble. She suddenly felt a little self-conscious. Maybe that wasn't…maybe Tyler didn't want her to do that kind of thing. "Did you…like it?" she asked.

Tyler nodded once, then again, more vigorously. "I've been…um. I've thought about it. Before. Watching you."

He looked over at her, his expression unsure. But a wave of heat and lust rushed through Corinne at his words. "What else have you thought about?" she asked quietly.

He smiled at her. "I'll tell you at the cabin."

Eight

TYLER

I t was almost painful how hard Tyler was by the time they got to the cabin. He was one second away from throwing Corinne over his shoulder and running toward the bedroom. He couldn't decide if he wanted to fuck her brains out on the bed or watch her fuck herself on the bed. Probably both? He practically sprinted to the front door.

"What about our suitcase?" Corinne laughed from behind him.

"Later!" he yelled back. He grabbed the key from under the mat and unlocked the door. It was freezing inside…Corinne stepped in past Tyler and shivered. She moved toward the thermostat and turned it up, and Tyler stepped up behind her and caught her waist. He buried his nose in her hair.

He was expecting her to turn around in his arms, but instead she pushed her ass up against him, rolling her hips. "Fuck," Tyler gritted out.

He could practically sense her grin. Who was this vixen in his arms? Tyler had always thought Corinne was the sexiest woman on the planet, but something had happened in the last two hours and now she was wielding her sex appeal like a weapon.

Which was so hot.

She rolled her hips again, rubbing against his hard cock. And he couldn't help it—he gripped her hips and tilted to grind into her. She let out a little noise of pleasure, so he did it again.

Part of Tyler wanted to take his time, but right now he just needed to be inside of her. He was desperate, aching, fumbling. He reached down and undid his zipper, pulling himself out of his briefs. He was about to yank Corinne's leggings down, but discovered that she had already done it. Her ass was full and bare in front of him, and he pumped himself once, groaning, barely controlling himself.

"Condom?" Tyler whispered.

Corinne shook her head and braced herself against the wall. "I just want to feel you inside of me," she said, her voice hungry. Tyler looked at her hands, fingers spread wide on either side of the thermostat. His eyes moved down to her arched back, her strong thighs—he knew from experience how strong those thighs could be.

"Tyler," his wife said. She was looking at him over her shoulder, her full red lips open, her eyes hungry. Tyler heard himself groan, then took his cock and plunged into her with so much force he lifted her onto her toes.

Corinne let out a cry.

"Okay?" Tyler asked hoarsely.

"Yes," Corinne gasped. When he didn't move, she balled her hands into fists. "Dammit, Tyler, fuck me. Please."

Tyler pulled his hips back and drove into her again, and she let out another cry. He suddenly realized how long it had been since they were able to be loud like this. The thought sent his movements into a frenzy, his hips bouncing against her, her cries getting higher and louder with each thrust.

Tyler was vaguely aware of a string of curse words he was letting out, but most of his concentration was on the heat of his wife's body, the slick perfection of it around him.

"Don't…stop…" Corinne gasped. Her moans were growing high-pitched, sounds Tyler recognized from a time before they had to worry about waking up the kids. He realized that his wife's fingers were moving quickly over her sex, bringing herself closer, and it was so hot that it took every ounce of willpower Tyler had to keep himself under control.

He didn't have to control himself much longer, though. Within seconds, Corinne's walls were shuddering around him, her legs shaking, her voice making a high, keening noise that was almost pornographic.

"Tyler," Corinne gasped, and that was all it took. Tyler's release pulsed through him, his hips bucking until he could barely stand upright. Tyler leaned forward and pulled his wife's back against his chest, whispering curses into her hair, one hand clutching at her breasts as he came down from his climax.

The two of them both leaned their hands against the wall, breathing heavily. Finally, he pulled out and walked to the bathroom to get Corinne a handful of tissues. When she had cleaned up, and when their clothes were more fully on again, they collapsed onto the couch together. Tyler wrapped an arm around his wife, and she draped her legs over his lap.

"Apparently we both needed that," he whispered.

Corinne let out a little laugh. "Apparently."

Now that Tyler wasn't completely distracted by how hot his wife was, he had an opportunity to look around the room. Sean's family had decorated it for the holidays, since they had family that used it fairly often.

Real pine boughs were hung on the walls, smelling woodsy and comforting, red ribbons tied in large bows at their centers. A large Christmas tree stood in front of the window, covered in ornaments and softly glowing lights. Stockings were hung on the mantle above the fireplace. A stack of firewood sat in a metal bucket nearby, ready to create a cozy blaze as night fell.

Tyler pointed to the thick white rug in front of the fireplace. "We should build a fire and have sex right there," he said.

Corinne grinned at him. "We absolutely should." She paused and then whispered, "You said you would tell me what else you've thought about. When we got to the cabin."

Tyler swallowed. "Well, watching you was definitely one of them."

"What else?"

Tyler looked over at his wife, suddenly feeling self-conscious. "It's dumb," he said.

Corinne shoved him playfully. "Come on, I wanna hear it," she said.

"Okay, but don't laugh," Tyler said. Corinne nodded, so he said quickly, "I'm some sort of repairman and you're an unsatisfied housewife who just needs me to help her out." He put air quotes around "help her out."

Corinne did laugh, but it was a joyful sound, not a dismissive one. It gave him the courage to keep talking.

"And this one isn't really realistic," he continued, "But doing it in the middle of some sort of apocalypse. Like we just fought off a bunch of zombies and we're all sweaty and in our shelter and then have wild sex."

"I like those fantasies," Corinne said, drawing a hand

down his chest. "And we can definitely make those happen. Or like, pretend to." She played with his belt buckle as she spoke. "Do you want to hear some of mine?"

Tyler thought of the list he'd found, the specifics of what she wanted him to do. "I um...I already read your list," he replied. "So I know them."

Corinne sat up and grinned at him. "Who says that was all of them?"

Tyler caught the mischievous gleam in her eye and damn, he was already getting hard again. "There are more?" he asked.

"One of them was—is—you watching me touch myself. And I kind of...I want to watch you touch yourself? Too?" Corinne suddenly seemed uncertain. "Is that weird?"

"First of all," Tyler said, "No, that's not weird. Second of all, I don't care if it is."

Corinne smiled. "And I want to do it with you in a swimming pool. I don't really know how to make that one happen, since we don't know anyone with a pool, but just keep it in mind."

He leaned forward and kissed along the side of his wife's neck. She smelled so good...familiar and warm and sweet, the brand of shampoo she'd been using for a decade filling him with longing. He moved his lips farther down, over her collarbones.

"Hey," she said softly.

Tyler stopped and looked up at her face. "Yeah?"

"I'm sorry I didn't tell you earlier how unhappy I was."

Tyler's stomach clenched with guilt. "You shouldn't have had to," he said. "I should have noticed. I don't know how I didn't."

"Still," Corinne said. "I kept a lot of what I was feeling

inside, waiting for you to notice. At a certain point, it was a little unfair to you."

"Well, I promise I'll try to pay better attention if you promise to tell me if something's bothering you."

"Deal," Corinne said with a grin. She leaned forward and kissed him, slow and deep. "I'm going to go take a shower. Can we continue this when I'm done?"

"Do you want company?" Tyler asked.

Corinne grinned, but shook her head. "Not this time. But that can definitely be on the table at some point. Right now I want to spend at least half an hour under hot water without a child interrupting me for something."

"I love you," he said.

She leaned forward and kissed him. "I love you, too," she replied. Then she stood and made her way to the bathroom.

Tyler told his dick to be patient, stood up, and then went and got their luggage from the car. He could hear the shower running in the other room, and he pictured his wife standing there, water running in drops and rivulets over her skin. He let out a little groan of desire.

It was still early, and he wasn't hungry, so instead he grabbed a towel of his own and went out onto the deck. The hot tub was blissfully steamy when he took the cover off. He didn't even bother putting a swimsuit on—the cabin was isolated enough, and he secretly hoped they'd be spending most of the next couple of days without their clothes on anyway.

He stripped down and sank into the water with a sigh. There was part of him that still felt guilty about the last few months. Last few years, really. He'd been such a shitty husband. He was probably going to accidentally be shitty again, but he was going to do his damnedest to keep those moments to a minimum. He was staring out at the trees, still thinking about how to do that, when he heard his wife call his name.

"Out here!" he called back.

Corinne stepped out onto the deck, a towel wrapped around her body, her hair wet over her shoulders. She smiled at him.

"How was your shower?" he asked.

"Heavenly," she replied.

"I know you just spent a lot of time in hot water," he said, "But care to join me?"

Tyler watched something pass over her face. Some anxiety caused her brow to furrow slightly.

"What is it?" he asked.

She looked at the hot tub and then back up at Tyler. "I…can't," she said.

Tyler frowned. "Why not?" he asked.

Corinne stared at the wood of the deck beneath her feet. "This isn't how I was planning on telling you this," she mumbled.

"Tell me what?" Tyler asked.

She looked up at him, and he couldn't read her expression. There was fear and hope and uncertainty. Tyler was getting nervous. He stood and stepped out of the hot tub, then put his hands on Corinne's upper arms. "What is it, honey?"

She smiled slightly at his nakedness, then looked up into his eyes.

"I'm pregnant," she said.

Nine

CORINNE

Tyler stood staring at her for a full thirty seconds. And those thirty seconds were terrifying. Was he happy? Scared? Angry? All of the above?

Just when Corinne was about to demand that Tyler please say something, his face broke into a grin. He wrapped his arms around her and pressed her to him. The water from the hot tub mingled with the water from her shower, both of them soaking the towel she had wrapped around her. She hadn't realized how cold the air on her skin was until Tyler pulled her against him.

"That's amazing," Tyler whispered. "Hon, that's amazing." He pulled back to look at her. "How long have you known?"

"I just took the test yesterday," she replied.

"Oh my god, is this why you've been sick?"

Corinne nodded.

"How do you feel?"

Corinne thought for a moment. "Honestly?" she said. "Exhausted? Terrified? Overwhelmed. And nauseous."

Tyler looked at her with concern. "Do you feel happy?"

She gazed up at her husband, his kind face, his warm eyes. And she realized that now that Tyler was showing up, now that they were reconnecting, she actually *was* happy. "Yes," she said.

"Good," Tyler replied, grinning. He pulled her into his arms again, and Corinne breathed in his familiar scent, layered with the slight chlorine smell of the hot tub.

"Like, I still don't know how we're going to do it," Corinne said into his skin. The cold air caused her to shiver slightly. "But if you're on my team, I think we can do it."

Tyler pulled away and cupped her face in his hands. "I'm on your team," he said. He leaned down to kiss her, slow and deep. Corinne opened her mouth to him, feeling heat gather in her core.

"I'm feeling really upset that I can't get into the hot tub with you right now," she whispered.

"How about we get into the bed instead?" Tyler replied.

"That'll work."

Corinne shed her towel and the two of them walked to the bedroom, their skin and hair still wet. She laid back onto the mattress and let Tyler move slowly up her body, touching, kissing, exploring. When he reached her head, he leaned down and whispered, "Do you want me to take my time?" He pressed a kiss to the sensitive spot beneath her ear, causing her back to arch. She nodded.

Until now, Corinne hadn't known that her hip bones were an erogenous zone. Or the arch of her foot. Or her knees. But as Tyler moved his lips and fingers over those parts of her, it was like her skin was waking up, her body aching for more of him.

She hadn't realized what Tyler meant when he said "take my time." He took more time than he ever had in their entire relationship. By the time she sank down onto him, she was already almost there. Her cry when she came echoed off the bedroom walls.

Twice.

~

Two months later

CORINNE STOOD from where she had been kneeling in the bathroom. She still had the occasional wave of morning sickness. (Or in this case, evening sickness.) Thank god it wasn't as bad as it had been in the first few weeks.

"Corinne?" Tyler called out.

"In the bathroom!" Corinne replied.

Tyler stepped into the doorway, Mason on his hip. "Hey, you okay?"

"Just the usual," Corinne said. "What's up?"

Tyler grinned at her. "This little guy wanted to tell you something."

"I pooped in da potty!" their toddler yelled.

"Oh my god! Good job!" Corinne never realized how much of parenting was tied to someone else's bodily functions, but she was genuinely thrilled to hear this. She reached out to hug her son. "Did he go all by himself?" she asked Tyler.

"Didn't even tell me he needed to," Tyler answered. "Just walked into the bathroom, did his thing, and came out to tell me about it."

"I'm so proud of you, baby!" Corinne said. She looked at her husband with relief. "Only one size of diapers at a time."

"Living the dream," Tyler replied, grinning. He turned to their son and started walking toward the kitchen. "Okay, buddy, let's get you a treat! Do you want Nutella or an Oreo?"

Corinne reached down to pet Pickle and Lulu. The two dogs had made a habit of accompanying her to the bathroom when she was sick, which was stressful at first, but now it was comforting. She pulled out her phone to text Bri.

CORINNE: You're not going to believe this but Mason just pooped in the potty BY HIMSELF. UNPROMPTED.

Bri texted back almost immediately.

BRI: OMG THAT'S AMAZING GOOD JOB MASON!!!

It was nice to have the kind of friend who could celebrate your kid's pooping triumphs with you.

When Corinne got to the kitchen, Mason was eating an Oreo and galloping in circles around the dining room table, where Emily was writing something with a look of deep concentration on her face. Corinne's husband came up behind her, circling her waist with his arms. He kissed the side of her head.

"Should we take the tree down?" he asked.

Corinne glanced into the living room, where the Christmas tree still stood, lights blinking serenely in the evening light.

"I think it's probably time," Corinne said. "We don't need it anymore."

"It *is* almost March," Tyler said, a gentle laugh in his voice.

"It's just been a nice reminder," Corinne said.

"Of what?"

"Of this past Christmas. The one when you gave me the best gift ever, when I thought we were going to have to just 'make it through.'"

Tyler leaned forward to whisper in Corinne's ear. "Was the gift my fantastic dick?"

Corinne laughed. "Well, there *was* that," she replied. "But I meant…all of this. Showing up. Being a dad and a husband and a partner."

She felt Tyler swallow. "Corinne?" he asked quietly. She turned in his arms and put her hands behind his neck.

"Hmm?"

"If I hadn't…if Justin hadn't talked some sense into me, what…what would have happened?"

Corinne searched her husband's face. His eyes were filled with uncertainty, and probably a little bit of fear.

"I don't know," Corinne answered honestly. "I knew that what was happening was not sustainable, but I don't know if I had made any kind of…plan."

"If I fuck it up again—"

"Tyler—"

"Sorry, if I screw it up again, will you…please just tell me?"

Corinne smiled. "I wasn't correcting your swearing," she said. She glanced at their kids. "Although that's probably a good idea. I was going to tell you that so far, you're not…screwing it up again. But if you are, I'll tell you."

"Do you promise?"

Corinne stood on her tiptoes to kiss Tyler's lips. "I promise."

Tyler inhaled and kissed Corinne back, then pulled away to lean his forehead against hers. "No more of this 'just making it through' business."

She nodded.

"You're my *wife*," he said.

"And I *feel* like your wife."

They kissed until both Mason and Emily started yelling for them to stop, and then broke apart with mutual grins.

West Tindale, Montana
HALFWAY THROUGH THE HOLIDAYS
To footpaths
To Tindale National Park
SILVERVIEW WAY
Sullivan's Coffee
Hitching Post Hotel
(Shops)
Little Park Theatre
Jerry's Fly Fishing shop
The Bar
Merrel's Grocery Store
Dottie's Candy Shoppe
West Tindale Visitor's Center
PINE RIDGE AVE
City Park
Pages & Pasta
(Shops)
Dairy Queen
Zhaos' Lucky Dragon
Real Estate Office
(Shops, incl the knife shop)
West Tindale Adventure Co
OLDVIEW WAY
5TH AVE
West Tindale School Field
West Tindale School
Wick & Bubble
(Shops)
Happy Bear Restaurant
Happy Bear Hotel
Clinic
Post Office
4TH AVE
(Homes)
Richland's Auto Repair
7 Eleven
Happy Home Trailer Park
Smith's Hardware Store
Movie Theatre
3RD AVE
SILVERVIEW WAY
(Apartments)
CVS
Holiday Inn
Ruby's Restaurant
GRIZZLY WAY
Library
Hungry Wolf Pancake House
TINDALE WAY
(Homes)
OUTPOST WAY
Rental cabins
2ND AVE
Little Tindale Inn
KOA
Church in the Pines
(Homes)
1ST AVE
American Horseback Adventures
West Tindale City Offices
(Homes)
Corinne & Tyler's house
West Tindale cemetery
To Silver Falls

Tindale National Park

HALFWAY THROUGH THE HOLIDAYS

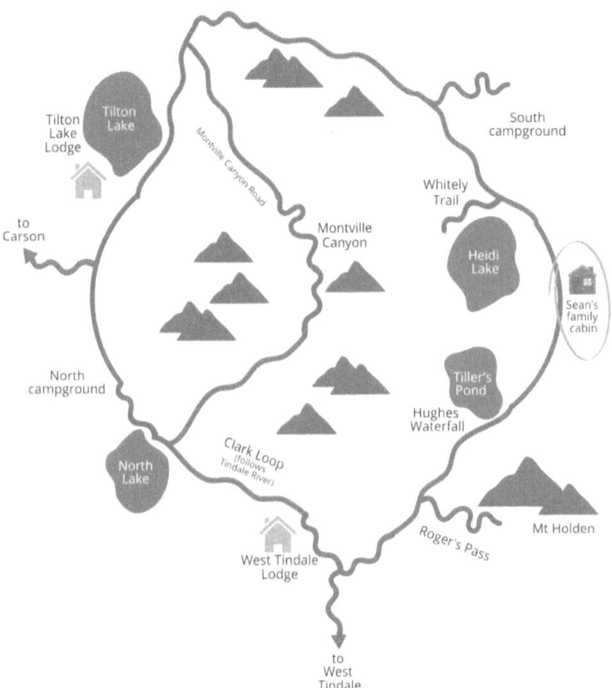

NOTE ABOUT INDIGENOUS HISTORY

Tindale National Park is a fictional place, based loosely on Yellowstone National Park in Wyoming and Montana. Indigenous peoples lived in that area for centuries before Europeans explored and named specific locations. Yellowstone was home to the Newe Sogobia (Eastern Shoshone), Cayuse, Umatilla, Walla Walla, Apsàalooke (Crow), and Tsètho'e (Cheyenne) peoples.

If Tindale National Park were a real place, it would likely share a similar history of colonization. The names of mountains, lakes, and other features would be the result of European occupation.

Out of respect for indigenous peoples, I did not wish to create an artificial Native American history for Tindale National Park to acknowledge. But I also did not want the history of colonization in this country to go unacknowledged.

I encourage readers to research the indigenous peoples who lived and continue to live in the places you call home.

Acknowledgments

Special thanks to Carleigh, Cathy, Ellie, Sam, Dan, Mikah, and Sheldon for being wonderful beta readers—your perspective made this story more full and grounded.

Special thanks to meine Oma, whose financial generosity gave me a little extra time for writing. Ich liebe Dich.

And love always to everyone who has embraced West Tindale and encouraged me to keep writing.

Also by Elle Whittaker

WEST TINDALE

Halfway to You

Halfway Across the Street

ROCK ROMANCE

Rules Worth Breaking

Kisses Worth Waiting For

ENCOUNTERS

Under His Hands

At Your Service

OTHER THINGS

Jane Eyre and Zombies

About the Author

Elle Whittaker is the pen name for Liz Whittaker, who is the daughter of a poem and an ancient Egyptian hieroglyph. She spent most of her time on the shores of Neverland before moving to Salt Lake City, where she currently lives in a library until she can afford an RV. Her heart alternates between pumping lemonade and ink. Her favorite foods are music and knowledge, which she eats as often as possible from atop her mountain of crippling student debt. Her other job is theatre. In her free time, she enjoys hugging trees, cross-stitching, and thinking about outer space. She is happily a victim of the kind of moon-struck madness that drives her to not only write romance novels, but poetry, scripts, essays, and theatre reviews under various names.

instagram.com/ellewhittakerromance
tiktok.com/@elle.whittaker.romance